HELPING YOUR BRAND-NEW READER

Here's how to make first-time reading easy and fun:

▶ Read the introduction at the beginning of each story aloud. Look through the pictures together so that your child can see what happens in the story before reading the words.

▶ Read the first page to your child, placing your finger under each word.

▶ Let your child touch the words and read the rest of the story. Give him or her time to figure out each new word.

▶ If your child gets stuck on a word, you might say, *"Try something. Look at the picture. What would make sense?"*

▶ If your child is still stuck, supply the right word. This will allow him or her to continue to read and enjoy the story. You might say, *"Could this word be 'ball'?"*

▶ Always praise your child. Praise what he or she reads correctly, and praise good tries too.

▶ Give your child lots of chances to read the story again and again. The more your child reads, the more confident he or she will become.

▶ Have fun!

Text copyright © 2002 by Margaret Park Bridges
Illustrations copyright © 2002 by Janie Bynum

First edition 2002

Library of Congress Cataloging-in-Publication Data

Bridges, Margaret Park.
Edna Elephant / written by Margaret Park Bridges ;
illustrated by Janie Bynum. — 1st ed.
p.   cm — (Brand new readers)
Summary: Edna the elephant dances,
tries on her new coat, starts to bake some cookies,
and arranges flowers in a vase.
ISBN 0-7636-1555-2
[1. Elephants — Fiction.]
I. Bynum, Janie, ill. II. Title. III. Series.
PZ7.B7619 Oo 2002
[E] — dc21   2001035067

2 4 6 8 10 9 7 5 3 1

Printed in Hong Kong

This book was typeset in Letraset Arta.
The illustrations were done in
digital ink and gouache.

Candlewick Press
2067 Massachusetts Avenue
Cambridge, Massachusetts 02140

visit us at www.candlewick.com

EDNA ELEPHANT

CANDLEWICK PRESS
CAMBRIDGE, MASSACHUSETTS

Margaret Park Bridges ILLUSTRATED BY **Janie Bynum**

Contents

EDNA DANCES

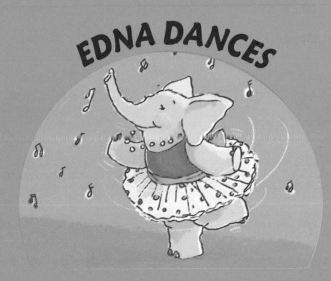

Introduction

This story is called *Edna Dances.* It's about how Edna dances to the music on her radio. She stands on one foot and bends her knees. When Edna leaps, she crashes to the floor.

Edna turns on the radio.

She sings.

She opens her arms.

She stands on one foot.

She spins.

8

She bends her knees.

9

She leaps.

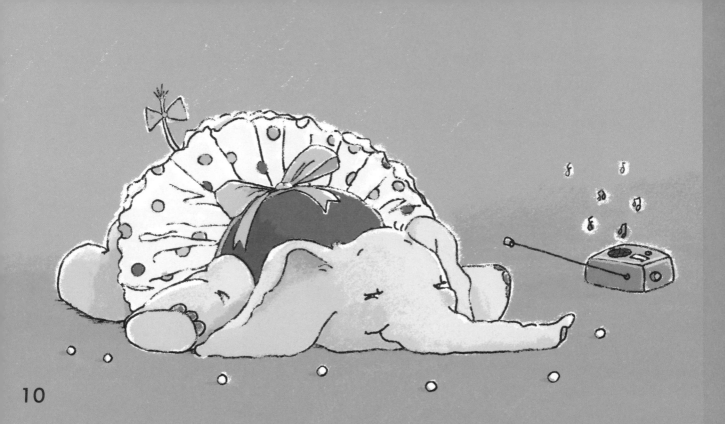

10

CRASH!

EDNA'S NEW COAT

Introduction

This story is called *Edna's New Coat*. It's about how Edna buttons her coat. As she buttons each button, her coat gets tighter. When she has buttoned the last button, they all pop off.

13

Edna puts on her new coat.

14

She buttons a button.

15

She buttons another button.

She buttons ANOTHER button.

She buttons the last button.

Edna's new coat is too tight.

POP! POP! POP! POP!

19

20

Edna's new coat is just right.

EDNA BAKES COOKIES

Introduction

This story is called *Edna Bakes Cookies.* It's about how Edna tries to make cookies and what happens when she tastes the batter.

Edna puts butter in the bowl.

She puts sugar in the bowl.

25

She puts flour in the bowl.

26

Edna stirs the batter.

She tastes the batter.

She tastes **MORE** batter.

29

Edna licks the spoon.

No more batter!

EDNA'S FLOWERS

Introduction

This story is called *Edna's Flowers.* It's about how Edna cuts the stems of some flowers to make them fit in a vase. When Edna makes the flowers too short for her vase, she puts them in her hat.

33

Edna puts the flowers in a vase.

34

The flowers are too tall.

Edna cuts the flowers.

36

The flowers are too short.

37

Edna gets another vase.

The flowers are too tall.

Edna cuts the flowers.

Edna puts the flowers in her hat.